Wind Over Dark Tickle

Heather Walter and Eric West

Illustrations by Sylvia Ficken
Songs by Eric West

produced by QLF/Atlantic Centre for the Environment

BREAKWATER

BREAKWATER
100 Water Street
P.O. Box 2188
St. John's, NF
AIC 6E6

QLF/Atlantic Centre for the Environment and Breakwater Books Ltd. gratefully acknowledge the financial support of the Fortis Education Foundation, the Human Resources Development Agreement, and the Government of Canada through the Canadian Studies Directorate.

Canadian Cataloguing in Publication Data

Walter, Heather, 1959-

    Wind Over Dark Tickle

    ISBN 1-55081-126-6 (bound)

    ISBN 1-55081-132-0 (pbk)

1. Marine ecology — Juvenile literature. 2. Marine resources — Juvenile literature. I. West, Eric. II. Ficken, Sylvia Quinton.
III. Title.

QH541.5.S3W35 1996   j574.5'2636   C96-950184-6

DEDICATION

For the children and fishing families of Newfoundland and Labrador.

SPLAT, SPLOSH, SPLAT.

Peter splashed water every which way as he marched in his boots along the edge of the ocean. The sea was grey, the sky was grey.

He shouted angrily across the wide water, "I hate Dark Tickle! And I hate you, boring ocean!" But his voice was lost on the wind.

The sea was tossing and turning, rolling and churning. Its fish were now so few there were hardly any at all. Its waters felt dirty and oily. The puffins and gannets and the other seabirds were flapping about this way and that in search of food.

Suddenly the sea noticed Peter. It tumbled and churned its waves up onto the shore. It took a deep breath and blew a strong wind towards Peter, calling, "Please...What is wrong with me? Where have my fish all gone?"

Peter heard only the whooshing sound of the waves and felt the wind ruffle his hair and tickle his cheeks. A big wave rolled in and he wasn't quick enough to avoid getting water right down inside his boots. Hey!

SLURP, SPLOTCH, SQUELCH.

His feet were wet but he didn't mind. Peter let the waves chase him…in and out and faster and higher and….

Suddenly he spied something Lying high and dry above the landwash—the biggest shell he had ever seen. He picked it up and turned it over and over in his hands. He put the shell to his ear and sat down with amazement at the sounds coming from inside. Sounds of the sea! Peter closed his eyes and lay back on the sand.

"Ah!" said the sea. "I'll lull him to sleep and sing to him in a dream."

Where have the fish all gone?
Are they hidden where I cannot see?
Or have they swum away, to come another day,
O now won't you please tell me?

When Peter woke up the song was washing 'round and 'round in his head.

"Hmmmm, where have the fish all gone?" he asked himself. He didn't know the answer to the sea's question, but he was very curious. Maybe someone in Dark Tickle could help. He picked up the shell and started to run back towards the village.

SLURP, SPLOSH, SQUELCH, SLURP, SPLOSH, SQUELCH.

Oops, his boots were still full of water! Peter laughed out loud as he stopped to wring out his soggy socks.

When he reached the first house, he met Mrs. Dooley, one of the oldest people in all of Dark Tickle. She was hanging her clothes out to dry. Peter stopped beside her and waited while she finished pinning up a pillowslip.

"Mrs. Dooley, can you tell me what happened to the fish in the sea?" The wind blew a gust that made the clothes on the line go flap, flap, flap.

Mrs. Dooley paused and looked way off over the ocean. "I can't say really," she answered at last. "But there was a time, many many years ago when I used to stand on this same porch and watch the dories coming in, right flat on the water, loaded full of fish. We only had rowboats and sailboats in those days. All hands would have to scramble. It was hard work, but good work."

It was almost as if she was hearing something. "Oh, there were plenty of fish then. And there were songs, songs we sang about all the fish we caught."

O, there's lots of fish in Bonavist' Harbour
lots of fish right in around here;
Boys and girls are fishin' together,
Forty-five from Carbonear!

CHORUS
Catch ahold this one, catch ahold that one
Swing around this one, swing around she
Dance around this one, dance around that one
Diddle dum this one, diddle dum dee.

Mrs. Dooley put a wrinkled hand on Peter's shoulder and said, "I remember the first motorboat that came to Dark Tickle. What a racket that was. And what a change. Pretty soon everyone had motorboats. Then they got bigger boats and faster boats. And since then they've got boats so big they've got fish plants right on board. They can stay at sea for months and catch all the fish they can find. Seems they were catching the fish before they hardly had a chance to grow."

Mrs. Dooley popped into her house and came out again with a plate of warm delicious-smelling chocolate chip cookies. She held them out saying, "Help yourself, Peter. It's hard to say where the fish have all gone. That's a tough question you've set out to answer. Nothing like a cookie or two to help you on your way."

Peter smiled and thanked her. He took two cookies and his seashell and headed on his way again.

*H*e hadn't gone far when he saw his friend, Sarah, sitting all alone under a big tree. She didn't look very happy.

"What's wrong, Sarah?", asked Peter.

"I just found out that I'm going to have to move away. I don't want to leave Dark Tickle."

Peter sat down beside Sarah and gave her one of his cookies. "Why do you have to go?" he asked.

"Father says there are no fish for him to catch and no other work for him here. And mom lost her job when the fish plant closed down. They say they'll have a better chance of getting jobs in a city somewhere."

"But there'll be movie theatres and swimming pools and stadiums and lots of fun things in the city."

"But Peter, I can't imagine not living by the sea. If you can keep a secret, I'll show you my favourite place in the cove."

Sarah pulled Peter up and together they ran through Dark Tickle and down to the shore.

Come with me to my home by the sea:
We can learn how to swim
With the whales and the otters;
In the cove where the wind never blows,
And everyone knows there are lots of things to do
Among the rocks and the sand,
If you give me your hand,
I'll take you to my home down by the sea.

CHORUS
Come with me, down to the sea;
Everywhere you'll find
That we're happy all the time,
Leave your troubles far behind
When you come to my home down by the sea.

Every day we'll go out on the bay
And we'll see all our friends
Who are playing in the ocean;
Take a ride on a fast-turning tide
Far and wide, we'll go drifting in and out
Among the rocks and the shore,
If you want to explore,
Then come to my home down by the sea.

When it was finally time for Sarah to go home, Peter realized that he'd never asked her the sea's question about the fish. But somehow it didn't matter.

As she started to leave, Peter thanked Sarah for sharing her special place with him. He picked up his seashell, and held it close to his ear as he headed up the beach again.

*U*p ahead he saw a young woman wading in and out, up and down, in the shallow water along the shore.

As he got closer he saw that she was wearing a rubber suit and carrying a dip net, scooping things out of the water. Whatever she scooped up she examined very closely.

He called out, "Excuse me, what are you doing?"

The young woman raised her head and smiled. She waded ashore and held the net out for Peter to have a closer look. "See what's inside," she pointed out, "well, those are baby fish. I'm collecting and counting samples of them. We are trying to figure out how many fish are out there."

Peter asked her, "Do you know a lot about the sea?"

"Well, I'm learning all the time," she replied. "I'm studying marine biology. I want to learn all I can about fish and all the things that affect life in the ocean."

He asked, "Uh, can you tell me, where have the fish all gone?"

"That's a good question. Every year there seems to be fewer and fewer of them. We don't know why exactly. All I can tell you is that these little fish have a tough life ahead. And unfortunately we know a lot more about how to catch fish then we do about the fish themselves. I'm afraid that we've been catching too many fish for too long."

She took the handle of her dipnet and drew a big bunch of dots in the sand. She said, "You see, if these are fish eggs, only a few will survive to become adults." She drew two large fish in the sand beside the eggs. "But these big fish can produce more eggs and the whole process can start again." She made a circle joining the eggs and the fish. "So, you see, if we are careful not to catch too many fish, there should be plenty to go around for ever and ever."

She smiled. "I hope you'll come down here and join me sometimes. The ocean needs all the help it can get!"

Peter thanked her. He tucked the shell under his arm and headed back towards Dark Tickle again.

*H*e was thinking about all the things he wanted to tell the sea when he saw a group of people trying to push a boat down a slipway into the ocean. He recognized his fisherman friend, Tom O'Brien. This was the boat Tom had just finished building. Peter ran over to pitch in. They all pushed and pushed. But the boat wouldn't budge until Tom began to sing, and then everyone joined in and pushed in time with the song…

I've worked all the winter and built a fine boat
(With a heave ho, lend me a hand)
She's built very sturdy, I think that she'll float
(With a heave ho, let's do what we can!)

They say that our codfish have all gone away
(With a heave ho, lend me a hand)
But I think that they'll be returning one day
(With a heave ho, let's do what we can!)

And when there are plenty of fish to be found
(With a heave ho, lend me a hand)
Then out on the ocean, that's where I'll be bound
(With a heave ho, let's do what we can!)

Finally the gleaming white boat slid down the slipway and into the water. Everyone clapped and shouted with excitement. It was the first new fishing boat that had been built in Dark Tickle in a long, long time and everyone was happy to see it floating on the harbour.

Peter suddenly realized how hungry he was, so he waved goodbye and headed home. His mother gave him a big hug and kissed his salty forehead. She noticed his seashell and said with a grin, "Looks like you had an adventure or two today!"

As they sat eating supper together, Peter talked excitedly about everything he'd done that day.

He talked and he talked and he talked until he could hardly keep his eyes open.

He barely even remembered climbing up the stairs and snuggling into bed. But just before drifting off to sleep, he remembered the seashell. He placed it on the pillow beside him. And sure enough, just as he'd hoped, the sea came to him again in a dream song.

Sleep my child, now close your eyes,
And I will sing you a lullaby;
The wind is still and the moon shines bright,
My waves will lull you all through the night.

CHORUS
Roll the waves ever gently,
Rocking the boats on the bay;
Soon the night will be over,
And the sun will begin a new day.

The moon is rising far overhead,
The birds are sleeping down in their beds
The whales and fishes are singing their song
As softly my waves will roll the night long.

*A*nd in his dream, Peter told the sea all that he had learned that day. He told of old Mrs. Dooley who had talked about the big ships, of Sarah who loved the sea but had to leave it behind, of the young woman who studied how the fish live, and of Tom O'Brien who built his boat and was determined to make his living from the sea again. He told the sea that even though there weren't many fish now, there were a lot of people who cared. And if we were careful, in time, the fish would come back.

Outside in the dark night, the sea grew calm.

When Peter awoke in the morning, he looked out his bedroom window and saw the sea gleaming like glass in the sunshine. Out of the corner of his eye, he caught the glimmer of the seashell lying on his pillow. And suddenly he thought of Sarah. Whenever she missed the sea, she could hold the shell to her ear and listen to the soothing sound of the wind and the waves. No matter how far away, she would be able to hear all the songs of the sea.

Smiling to himself, Peter dressed quickly and ran downstairs. In the early morning sun, with the beautiful shell tucked under his arm, he ran through the village all the way to Sarah's house.

A soft warm wind blew over Dark Tickle.

See the sun is rising
and the storms have gone away.
Seagulls circle in the air
and welcome in the day;
The fishing boats are leaving now
and heading out to sea,
To hear them sounding once again
brings happiness to me.

CHORUS
The sea becomes a part of you,
As it is part of me;
For it has made us what we are,
And what we'll come to be.

The sea is calm and peaceful now,
not troubled as before;
People come from all around
to gather on the shore;
They bow their heads in gratitude
for all the sea has done,
Giving life to everything
and hope to everyone.

ACKNOWLEDGEMENTS

This project came about with the help of many people. We would like to give special thanks to Jan Andrews for editing the manuscript and to Al Pittman for his insightful comments. Nora Lester and Margie McMillan of Granny Bate's Children's Bookstore in St. John's gave us valuable advice throughout the writing process. Many friends also encouraged us along the way, and we'd especially like to acknowledge the contributions of Helen Peters, Patrick McCloskey, Antje Springmann, Vickie Walsh, and Larry Jackson.

We field-tested the story and songs with primary and elementary school children along Newfoundland's southwest coast, from Port aux Basques to Rose Blanche; we thank them and their teachers for greeting us warmly and for discussing issues surrounding the fishery from their perspective. We are also grateful to Barry LeDrew and Harry Elliott at the Department of Education for their encouragement and feedback regarding links with the curriculum.

QLF/Atlantic Centre for the Environment produced this book in association with Breakwater Books. On their behalf and ours, we are very grateful for the funding support received from the Fortis Education Foundation. Sharon McLennon and the Fortis Board of Directors showed a real vision for education, and we appreciate the commitment they made to this project. We also acknowledge the support of the Cooperation Agreement on Human Resource Development, and the Government of Canada through the Canadian Studies Directorate.

We are very grateful for Breakwater Books' dedication and enthusiasm towards this project. Thank you to Clyde Rose and his staff, particularly Laura Woodford, Carla Kean, Nadine Osmond, and Krista-Lee Goulding for molding a beautiful book from an idea—and for continuing to believe in it. And to Clyde, for proposing the title that we just couldn't let blow away. A special thanks goes to Sylvia Ficken, who adopted Peter and his story and brought him to life with her beautiful illustrations. We are honoured that she lent her imagination to our project.

And finally, we would like to thank the children we have met in our performances across Newfoundland and Labrador and elsewhere in eastern Canada; they continue to inspire us with their joy of life and their hope for the planet. We are in good hands.

Heather Walter and Eric West

CONTRIBUTOR BIOGRAPHIES

Heather and Eric

Heather Walter and Eric West have been performing music together since 1988—in schools, concert halls, festivals, as well as on radio and television. They have recorded two children's albums, and have toured extensively throughout Canada.

Heather and Eric have co-produced several environment and music television specials with CBC. The first of these, "No Small Wonder" won a North American Film and Video Award from the Outdoor Writers Association of America. They have also been featured on Sesame Street Canada since 1991 on a series of marine education music videos entitled "Creatures at Home in the Sea". Their commitment to weaving environmental themes into their music was rewarded in 1994 when they were presented with the Newfoundland and Labrador Environment Award.

For more information, contact:
> "Heather and Eric", North by East Productions
> 65 Colonial Street, St. John's, Newfoundland, A1C 3N2
> (709) 722-0966

Sylvia Ficken

Sylvia Ficken (nee Quinton) grew up in Princeton, a small community in Bonavista Bay on the east coast of Newfoundland. She now resides in Topsail, Newfoundland with her husband, her sons and her two cats.

The Quebec Labrador Foundation
(Atlantic Centre for the Environment)

The Quebec Labrador Foundation is a private, not-for-profit conservation and educational organization incorporated in Canada and the United States. The organization conducts programs primarily in rural areas throughout eastern Canada and northern New England in conservation, education, and community development. The Atlantic Centre for the Environment conducts the foundation's environmental programs.

For more information, contact:
> QLF/Atlantic Centre for the Environment
> 1253 McGill College Ave., Suite 680
> Montreal, Quebec, H3B 3Y5
> (514) 395-6020